# What Makes a Witch

## Linnea Capps

Weasel Press

What Makes a Witch
Linnea Capps

ISBN-13: 978-1-948712-60-6

© 2020 Linnea Capps

Weasel Press
Lansing, MI
http://www.weaselpress.com

*To Ayla, So that you may know no matter what you discover about yourself during life's adventures, your mother will always find you magical.*

# What Makes a Witch

Content warnings for this book can
be found on page 50

1

Greer groaned, a weak and pathetic sound drowned out by the many footsteps stirring dust and the cacophony of conversations found in the lower marketplace. The hard ground offered as little comfort as the stone wall he found himself curled up against. Even if someone had heard the sound, no one would have paid him any mind.

He had learned during his first days of begging that he would simply be laughed away. Those he had tried to ask may not have been cats, but the hares, marmots, and gophers still considered themselves too high of class to be seen interacting with a rat. Not to mention a rat in the ridiculous attire he had been forced to run away wearing.

Greer also knew there was no hope to be had with his own kind. Most rats considered every mouth but their own competition. With limited food, adults would often eat before the children so that they may be strong enough to work for more. Or so they could scrape together just enough for a fix of addictive poppy wine so many craved. Pups rarely were seen laughing or playing. Most sat quietly, ears downturned. The tails of those who walked trailed in the dirt to conserve any bit of energy they had.

Even if the desperate culture of his brethren wasn't an obstacle, he was positive his father would have told anyone who would listen of his son's shame. He had even attempted to scrounge in the garbage of several restaurants before the feline guards had run him off with threats of violence. Even the trash of the higher class seemed to be too good for rats like Greer in their eyes. While their species were different, they all walked on two legs just the same. Greer didn't understand why it mattered.

After the first days, the pain in his belly had lessened, but Greer became worn and listless. The relief he found was only temporary: the pain quickly came back with a vengeance when his incredibly limited stores of fat had been eaten away.

So there he sat, exhausted, attempting to distract himself by listening to the numerous exchanges taking place around him. While the fog of malnourishment clouded his mind, squeaking tones of a begging shopkeeper managed to break through.

"My apologies. I thought they were one of the coven!"

Greer tilted his head toward the sounds, spotting

a stern-looking hare, a large footpaw tapping impatiently in the dirt as she stared down a frazzled marmot in front of his stall. Her fur was a mottled brown that looked light compared to her black-as-night gown. Seeing how fine the cloth was, with its accents made of an equally black lace, there could be no mistake: this woman was a witch!

"Anyone can wear a gown; that so-called witch you sold to has been exiled from Eastaughffe by the Grand Coven!"

"Yes Mistress Charlotte, please forgive me!"

The hare's foot increased its tapping pace as she glared down at the shopkeeper. Greer knew the members of the Grand Coven held much sway in the kingdom as sworn protectors of the realm. Witches did not often come to the slums, and he had never seen one that was a rat like him. Witches would take worthy apprentices to pass down the arts, with those deemed worthy more often than not coming from the upper class.

"I might be swayed to not mention your indiscretion to Mistress Elizibeth...if in return you tell other merchants that this woman is not to be trusted. She always walks with that gnarled wooden walking stick; she's easy enough to spot. It's not like we have many ferrets living here either."

"Yes, Mistress Charlotte! I will tell anyone that listens!" The merchant bowed his head in reverence to the hare who stood before him. Greer eyed the rabbit who had her ears turned back with concern.

"See that you do..."

She quickly turned to walk away from the marmot, who kept his head bowed until she was far from his sight.

Greer puzzled over the interaction. An exile of the Grand Coven? Few were foolish enough to become an enemy of the witches, let alone having them use their sway with the king to actually ban them from access to the town where the coven was based.

His thoughts were interrupted by a growling from his stomach. The conversation had been curious, but it could only distract him so long. He almost considered rushing toward where Mistress Charlotte had been walking. Witches were not only sworn to protect the realm, but to help those who resided in it.

Despite that, he had only ever seen this in practice the rare times witches came to the slums in attempts to quell outbreaks of disease. Furthermore, hares held a much higher place in society than rats; he'd likely be swatted away as he had been before.

Still, Greer knew the situation was grave. Without some sort of help or food soon, he knew he would lose any strength he had left. After that, it wouldn't be much longer before he would have nothing to worry about ever again. It would be impossible to worry once he was dead.

A desperation-fueled idea sparked a thought within his hunger-addled mind. Yes, no one of a higher class would help him, but what about someone who was as ostracized as he was? What about an exiled witch?

His body ached in protest as he rose to his feet paws, trudging away from the market to make his way to the outskirts of town. He thought if anyone could somehow survive outside the city limits, they must have set themselves up in the forest. It was a gamble, but the entire idea was a gamble in the first place. Not succeeding meant starving for sure; at least the forest might have berries he could try to find at the worst.

After several looks of general confusion and disgust in his direction and at least an hour of exhausted trudging, he finally found himself on the outskirts of Eastaughffe. The town rested between two massive hills, the Holt and the Fell, with a valley to one side that led towards the forest, the other paths to other towns. Greer stood before the tall grass that lay between himself and the thicket of trees, attempting to summon the courage he would need.

## 2

"Oy pup!"

The hunger had finally driven him to hallucination; he was sure of it. The soft feminine chitter he heard couldn't be real. He had just been imagining his mother too powerfully.

"Ah don't wish ta startle ya pup, but ya need ta eat. Up wit' ya!"

Greer felt his body shake gently. Eat? Wait, where was he? His paws flexed weakly to find what felt like wooden armrests beneath them. Was he sitting? Groggily, he forced his eyes open.

The ferret that stood before him had white fur tinged almost as if with ash in small places. It clashed against the black of her simple gown. Her eyes were an earthy brown that accentuated the soft features of her maw, the pink of her nose. She was smiling encouragingly, ears perked and excited.

"Good, you're wakin'! When I found ya collapsed in th' woods in 'at frock I honestly thought ya dead! I'll get ya some stew, yeah?"

Greer blinked. Why had he gone into the forest? He felt as though his brain were coated in thick mud, making the escape of any clear thoughts difficult. He allowed his eyes to close once again, trying his best to remember.

He had tried to find an exiled witch in the forest. He faintly remembered trying to search for paths of trampled undergrowth, meandering without any sense of direction. He realized he must have passed out from hunger and was later found by the ferret.

"Here ya are, pup! Stingin' nettle soup. Healthy, get yer feet kickin' again!"

Greer eyed the food, the emerald green not a color he was accustomed to seeing in a soup. Still, he could see the steam rising from the bowl, and it smelled pleasantly of herbs.

He was positive this woman must be the witch to be feeding him this way. His gamble had somehow paid off, and he wasn't about to question this sudden good fortune.

"Thank you, Mistress...?" Greer let his voice trail off, hoping she would reply.

She cocked up an amused ear. "Mistress? Now that's na a title I hear oft'n! I like it! So Mistress Addison ta ya, pup."

He nodded, a growl from his stomach causing a powerful pang of discomfort. Ignoring the spoon, he brought the entire bowl to his maw, desperate to gulp down any nourishment he could manage.

"Oy! Slow down pup, or it'll jist come back up!"

It mentally pained him beyond belief to slow down the eating his body was screaming at him for, but he listened to her advice. He didn't want to lose the most food he had eaten in weeks by retching on the ground from an upset stomach.

He sipped slowly, taking a moment to gain bearings of his surroundings. He sat in a comfortable chair, the tattered clothes he had been wearing gone, replaced with a simple black cloak that was too large for him, obviously originally fitted to his host. He was briefly mortified, remembering just exactly what he had been wearing, and even more so that she had likely seen him naked when changing him.

His body was covered in a warm quilt, only his arms sticking out so that he could eat. Even such a small use of energy as holding the bowl soon made him grow weary.

"Mistress Addison, I'm too tired to eat more. I'm sorry..." His voice trailed in a drowsy stupor.

The ferret smiled and gently took back his bowl, setting it aside. "Never mind, take plenty time ta rest. Th' soup won't grow legs an' run anyways. Ye can have more when yer ready aye?"

Greer thought he had responded but couldn't be sure with how quickly his body called for him to slumber. His eyes closed once more, and the embrace of sleep took him.

## 3

Greer had been with Mistress Addison for a few days and had begun to feel much better. It seemed that the ferret never had a shortage of food, foraging for some sort of vegetables, berries, even roots from the forest to make him meals. His times spent awake had been filled with Mistress Addison humming unfamiliar tunes as she sewed him a simple tunic and trousers suited to fit his small frame. His strength had been returning, but he still found himself sleeping in until late morning to regain some of the energy he had lost.

This morning was different. A concussive burst of force boomed outside, punctuated by a loud crack of splintering wood. The sound snapped Greer awake. His claws sank deep into the wood of his chair, adrenaline pulsing through him from his terror. What could even make such a loud sound?

His head turned to search for Mistress Addison, but she was nowhere inside the hut. He had no one to protect him if whatever monster that raged outside came for him next. Witches may be tasked with protecting the realm, but whatever was causing these noises couldn't be something Mistress Addison should face alone. Greer fought against his fears, finding a sharp knife on a countertop and gripping it tightly in his paws.

Even in his current state, if Mistress Addison was in danger, he refused not to defend a woman who had offered such kindness to him. Cowardice would not win; he would try his best to fight and protect her.

Greer padded as quietly as he could muster towards the door, moving more deliberately than he ever had before in his life. He tried his best to steady the paw pushing that door open, hoping with every fiber of his being it wouldn't creak, giving away his position.

His luck held: the door pressed open just enough so he could slide his wiry frame through. He kept his back to the wall, inching closer to its edge, mentally urging himself on. His paw shook from fear and the tightness of its grip on the knife. The time had to be now; he turned the corner only to find...

It was Mistress Addison! Determination painted the ferret's features as she stood at a long distance from a mangled tree, panting from what seemed to be great physical exertion. She swiped her paws through the air as if scratching an invisible foe. With each sweeping of her paw came the otherworldly boom followed by splintering wood as claw marks appeared on what remained of the tree.

There were no strange creatures in sight. Greer then realized that, had Mistress Addison truly been under attack, he would have likely heard the sounds of her crying out for help. He felt a nervous agitation at the fact that he hadn't realized this sooner.

Just as quickly as those thoughts entered his mind, they vanished as another realization overcame him. Mistress Addison was performing magic! He had never seen true magic up close before, and his jaw dropped in awe at the mystical sight he paid witness to.

"Greer? Is 'at ya?"

The rat let out a surprised squeak at being noticed, realizing it may have been quite rude to be spying on her as he had. "Y-yes, it's me. I'm sorry to have disturbed you!"

The ferret let loose a boisterous laugh. "Ah should be th' body apologizin', ah likely woke ye up from a good nap! Ah just haven't had time ta practice since carin' for ye. Couldn't bide a second longer!"

Relief swept over Greer that he was not in any sort of trouble. He scampered over towards her, unable to contain his excitement. "I thought some monster was attacking; I even grabbed a kitchen knife!"

The comment earned him another raucous round of roaring in delight. "Oh, mah sweet innocent pup, if a monster was attackin', 'at knife woulda done as much good as a toothpick! Still, it's quite kin' ah ye ta care an' braver even 'at ya tried defendin' me."

Greer's ears turned back sheepishly, embarrassed at his feeble attempts at 'rescue'. Despite her teasing, he could sense a bit of pride from Mistress Addison from the bravery he had shown. He allowed it to bolster him, having rarely received such praise before in his childhood.

"So that's magic? You just turned an entire tree into kindling!"

"Aye it is! Truly though, it's na easy, it can be exhaustin'. Besides, it's the kin' ay magic best used only ta defend yourself. There's far better magics for learnin' in th' world."

The ferret slowly approached what remained of the tree, kneeling down and placing both of her paws on its stump. It seemed to Greer that she was trying her best to focus, but he wasn't sure on what. That was at least, until the tree started growing right before his eyes.

"W-What!"

Mistress Addison couldn't stop her tail from wagging in glee at his surprise as the tree began to retake its form, branches steadily reaching back towards the sky. Bark reforming around gashes like scabs over injured flesh. Soon the only way anyone could have known the tree had been damaged at all was the splinters previously carved magically from it scattered across the grass.

"Pup? Wee pup? Snap roarin' fu' an' fetch ma cane, would ye?"

Greer hadn't realized just how transfixed he was on the magic taking place before him. He shook his head as if it would clear the cobwebs in his mind before running back towards the hut. He returned the knife to the counter before retrieving Mistress Addison's gnarled wooden walking stick and hurrying back out to deliver it to her.

"Thank ye pup. That's th' most lively I've seen ya in days! It's good ta see ye on th' mend." The ferret was breathing hard. She clutched onto the cane as she rose to standing, teetering slightly in place.

It was obvious to Greer just how fatigued the magic had made her become, so he offered his arm to her paw not currently grasping the cane for support. She gladly accepted.

"I didn't know magic would exhaust witches that did it this way."

The ferret nodded, the two making their way back towards the hut. "It doesn't have ta. Ah clawed off far more than ah should have. Ah had wee left ta heal th' tree wi'."

Greer noticed her accent seemed to thicken with exhaustion, but he was so bursting to the brim with questions he wanted answered that he determined he could sort out anything she said. "Then why heal the tree? You could have just left it there."

Mistress Addison looked over at Greer thoughtfully. "There's na sense killin' somethin' just so ah can practice. Every life in the world, e'en a single tree, should be treated as important."

The two had approached the door, Greer taking in this bit of wisdom as Mistress Addison opened it. She settled into a corner filled with overstuffed pillows he had often seen her enjoy, and he moved to sit in what he had become accustomed to thinking of as his chair.

He allowed her a moment to relax before speaking.

"Could I learn to do that?"

Mistress Addison loosed a sorrowful sigh. "Pup, I would love ta, but there's jist a wee problem. Have ye ever seen a lad do magic?"

Greer thought of his small experience with witches. It did strike him that he hadn't ever seen a man tending to the sick of the slums. "No. I haven't met many witches though."

"Only a lass can control th' power of th' ley lines."

He was unsure if it was the ferret's thick accent or if he had simply never heard the word before, but he had no idea what a ley line might be. Greer's confusion was betrayed by the twitching of his nose and downturned ears that Mistress Addison easily noticed.

"Th' ley lines are invisible rivers ay magical power flowin' through th' land. Witches can feel them, call upon them ta heal or hurt, bend them ta their wills. If trained, they can sense 'at magic, feel it buzzin' through their bones n' souls!" A wind stirred suddenly as she spoke causing her fur and cloak to billow dramatically. Her eyes shone bright as she cracked a wide grin.

Greer's eyes widened in awe; Mistress Addison could control the elements themselves! Exhilaration overpowered any sense of calm, his tail lashing about. "If no one has trained a boy how would you know they couldn't do magic? Take me as an apprentice: I could be the first!"

The wind stopped as suddenly as it started. Mistress Addison's fur returning to its normal state, her ears drooping. "A lass connects ta th' Earth Mother in a way na' lad can. She births magic inta' th' world so only those 'at can give birth themselves can control th' power."

It sounded to Greer as though she was sarcastically quoting the last words she spoke. He suspected she didn't like whoever originally spoke them as she spat bitterly onto the earthen floor as if trying to get the taste of the words she had spoken out of her maw.

"You don't sound like you really believe that."

"Na' those exact words. Teachin' lads magic has been attempted in th' past. It has always failed. Truths cannot be denied."

The mournful look that painted the ferret's face could not stop his curiosity. The ability to control magic? It could change his life! What would it even be like? He quickly concocted a reasonable argument for him to learn it.

"I have no family to go back to. I have no skills, nor do I know a trade. Please? I could use purpose. It cannot hurt to try one more time."

Mistress Addison's tail swished through the air, her expression puzzled but curious. "Ah certainly don't wanna send ya away. You're a wee bit young ta be plyin' yer body as wares like ye were."

Plying his body as wares? Did she mean prostitution? Everyone knew some chose to sell intimate services as a career, but most considered anyone who did so the lowest caste of society. He had never understood why they were disparaged so. They needed to eat like everyone else and did what they had to so they could. He could find nothing wrong with that. Still, he had never lifted his tail for someone else's pleasure and the idea that Mistress Addison thought he had left him frustratedly flustered.

"I was doing no such thing!" His tail wagged furiously in annoyance as his species was known to do.

"Pure? Ah jist saw ye in 'at frock an' thought... Maybe a member of higher society wi' strange perversions... "

The ferret's voice trailed off, Greer easily able to tell what she had implied. The idea that a member of higher society would stoop so low as to force themselves upon a child in such a way deeply disturbed him. Besides, the dress he had been found in... That was a story he was not yet ready to share. He did appreciate the clothes the ferret had sewn for him, even though their rigid traditional style for young men was not to his taste.

"No. I was homeless and... It was all I had to cover myself at the time." It was a lie, his voice quavered as he told it.

"If ye say so, ah 'pologize for assumin'."

He felt certain she knew he hadn't been truthful, but was grateful it seemed she chose to allow him his privacy on the matter.

"Can ye read?"

Greer lowered his head, shaking it shamefully. Most of his kind only worked as physical laborers and had no need to read. He had once found a book for small children he had been fascinated with, but never knew the title.

He had found it on the streets one day, likely dropped and forgotten by a higher-class child who had accidentally found their way to the slums. He had taken it home, hiding it in the house as his greatest treasure. He was unable to understand the words, but he had always loved the pictures. A woman, a rat like him, was dressed in rags covered with cinder and soot. Though her family was mean to her, she stood strong, even sewing a dress so she could dance with a prince! Deep down, he had wished he could rise from where he was in such a way.

One day, however, his father had come home while he was enjoying his prized possession. His father had stolen it from his grasp, taking Greer by surprise. Upon seeing the pictures of the rat-turned-princess in the book, he had groaned, berating Greer for what he saw.

"You don't need no books! No one reads when they work in the mines like you will boy, especially not this sissy garbage!"

His father had thrown the book into the fire, his one escape from the world consumed in the flames that were supposed to warm him.

"No, Mistress, I don't know how to read..."

"Aye... Ah hoped ah cood teach ye ta heal wi' herbs at least, but 'at takes books. Ye cannot sense th' ley lines..."

"How do you know?" Greer was surprised that he spoke out with such confidence, but stood firm. "Can you show me what it feels like to find it? I could practice with that!"

"Listen pup, ah admire yer spunk but there's more to it than 'at. It's quite a feelin', th' lads 'at tried before gained a cravin' for it. Became addicted, couldn't stop searchin'. Is 'at something you're willin' ta risk?"

The idea gave Greer a moment of pause. An addiction? He had seen what poppy wine and other substances could do to those desperate for their next fix. Not just in strangers around, him but from his own father. You could turn cruel without reason, some would lie, cheat, or steal. Anything to get another taste.

The idea sickened him, but this was a chance at magic. To be able to claw down trees as he saw, heal those in need, maybe even change lives for all of the rats living in the slums. To his knowledge, he would be the first rat to ever use magic, a historic achievement that would surely be recorded! He couldn't turn down such an impressive opportunity.

"I can handle this, Mistress Addison. Please, just allow me to try!"

"All right, pup, if ye wish ta learn that badly, ye may. On three conditions. Ye will learn ta read, ye will learn ta write, an' ye must swear ta bide by th' Witch's Code as all apprentices do."

While he knew he was asking to learn magic, it hadn't occurred to him that request meant he would be become a full apprentice! He stood from his chair, showing determination as strongly as he could in every feature. This was his chance at an incredible future; he would not turn it down.

"I will, Mistress Addison!"

The ferret rose from the pillow mound without using a muscle, magic lifting her into the air. A gentle breeze flowed through the room. The softest tingle, not caused by the breeze, seemed to brush over Greer's fur. Was this what magic felt like?

"Greer, do ye swear ta adhere ta yer word as if it were iron? Ta strive na ta harm, but ta brin' joy inta the world?"

"I swear!"

"Ta act wi' dignity, courage, an' honour?"

"I swear!"

"Ta follow mah every instruction until such a time ye become a full witch yerself?"

"I swear!"

"An' above all else, do ye swear ta be true ta yerself?"

This final oath seemed much different than the others. It was easy to promise to keep his word and listen to what he was taught. What did it mean to be true to himself? Who was he truly inside? After his father had forced him from his home he was no longer sure. Still, he was determined to learn magic.

"I swear!"

Mistress Addison grinned in approval, reaching out her paws to gently cradle the rat's head. Greer's heart began to race with anticipation.

"This, pup, is magic, th' power of th' ley lines."

In the first moments, Greer felt nothing. Was it truly this hard to feel if you were a boy? Then the fire began blazing a trail through his veins. While it burned it caused no pain, and the sensation quickly turned to shockwaves of power rippling through his very form.

As quickly as the sensation overcame him, it left,

Mistress Addison removing her paws and leaning back with labored breaths.

"While it may be a hopeless cause, ye may learn th' ways ay magic. Congratulations... Apprentice Greer."

Greer was unable to contain his excitement. He flung himself forward, squeezing the ferret with all the might his tiny frame could muster.

"Thank you, Mistress Addison; that was incredible! I want to learn: how do I practice? Can you teach me now?"

"You're welcome pup, but calm! Ye ave' a first lesson! Ye felt what it was like, th' magic flowin' through ye? If ye fin' a ley line ye can feel th' same forces coursin' through it. Go outside an' try ta fin' a ley line ye can sense while ah cook us up some tatties an' neebs eh?"

Greer hadn't the faintest clue what sort of food 'tatties an' neebs' might be, but he was too excited to care. He released his mistress from her hug and rushed out the door, determined he would sense a ley line before they ate that night.

4

Unfortunately for Greer, he was unsuccessful in finding a ley line that night. Nor was he any more successful during any night of the following week. Each morning he would rise and enjoy whatever breakfast his mistress could make from ingredients in the forest before his lessons began. He struggled to learn letters so that he might be able to read, all the while distracted at the task he knew he would only gain permission to attempt before dinner. Searching for a ley line.

He tried to focus as his mistress would draw letters in the earth that made their floor, but he would catch himself glancing towards the sun, trying to figure out what time of day it might be. Every cool breeze, prickle across his skin, something rubbing against his fur, would give him a jolt of excitement that he had somehow gotten to feel the magic again.

Every time, however, he was disappointed this wasn't the case. Mistress Addison had required he only be allowed to search during dinner preparation to try and keep him from going overboard; she too worried about the potentially addictive nature of the hunt. The first two days he had been obedient towards this request, he had sworn to follow her every instruction.

Soon, he couldn't physically control the urge any longer. He would wait until Mistress Addison slept, sneaking outside under the cover of her loud snoring. Still, none of the additional searching helped him reach his goal.

He found himself so desperate that as the ferret released him while she made what she called 'Mushroom Surprise,' he found himself lying flat on the forest floor. Maybe, he had reasoned, if his entire body was touching the ground, his added closeness to the earth would allow him a better sense of the ley lines.

He groaned, allowing his face to rest gently against the dirt and grass below him. This, like many other decisions he had made lately, seemed to have been a terrible idea. Sure, coming into the woods had saved him from certain death from starvation, but now he sought the feeling of magic again so desperately, he felt as though every hour without its touch was agony. A feeling he was warned he could never escape unless he found the flow of a ley line.

He could have avoided this entire mess, been hungry but home, sharing some watered down soup with his mother and father had he also had the clear judgement to not try on that damn dress.

Greer tried to push the thoughts from his mind, but found no success. It dragged him back to that day every time he tried to find the ley lines. The day when he thought he had the house all to himself. One of his mother's dresses left lying on the floor, falling from her arms as she took clothes to the river to wash. He had always admired dresses, thought how wonderful it must feel to have them flowing in the breeze as one ran along.

He knew these weren't the thoughts most male pups would have but he couldn't help them. He had always been different, from wanting to read to the strange feelings he had always harborded over his body. Something had never felt quite right, but he had never been able to put a digit on it. He knew he couldn't dare tell his mother, who would likely tell his father. Without a steady supply of poppy wine, Greer knew the rage he would face from his father for being anything 'different' would be too much to handle.

Yet here he was, home alone with a chance to try on a single dress. No one would need to know, it could be his own secret. Just quickly put it on and just as quickly take it off, no harm done, right?

He hadn't managed to take it off quickly. Something about the soft fabric lying gently against his fur felt so right, he couldn't bring himself to. He swayed his hips, watching the fabric wave to match his movements. He had giggled, twirling in a circle to see how it would spin before stopping in his tracks. The magic he had felt nights before was reminiscent of the euphoria he felt in that moment. He could almost feel a tingling flowing through him before it felt as though lightning struck through him, reminding him of the sting of his father striking him across the maw.

"Greer, it's dinner time! Get some scrap pup!"

Mistress Addison's call snapped him back to reality. He was happy for the reprieve: he didn't wish to relive being told how he was 'a disgusting freak', the pain of being tossed out of the door onto the streets, and how he had been told to 'never come back unless you want every sissy bone in your body broken'. He sniffled softly, he had never gotten to say goodbye to his mother, and these were likely the last words he would ever hear a member of his family say.

"Oy pup, come on! While it's hot yeah?"

He decided that good food would chase away these blues and offer the best distraction from wanting to hunt further for the ley lines. He could not deny he had never eaten better in his life than since being found by his mistress. Her knowledge of edible plants and berries made for fantastic meals the likes of which he had never seen before.

He only found one problem at each meal. Mistress Addison would take a small black bottle, one of many she kept locked away on a high shelf, and take a swig before they began to eat. Normally, this would seem an honestly innocent gesture, but he knew what those bottles usually contained: poppy wine.

Greer had done his best to say nothing, appreciating the care he had been shown by Mistress Addison.

Today, however, the memories of his father fogged his judgement. Would he have been kinder had he never been addicted to the drink? What would happen if his mistress became the same way, would he be cruelly tossed back onto the streets?

Frustration at being unable to find a ley line quickly melded with the anger and fear he felt, causing him to blurt out, "How can you drink that garbage? I thought you were a better person than that!"

Mistress Addison froze, her eyes going as wide as her ears were alert. Greer was positive this was the first time he had seen anything close to anger in her expression. "Excuse me?"

"That bottle might be black to disguise what's inside, but I know that's just to hide the poppy wine!"

Mistress Addison slammed a paw down on the table. "'At is enough! Like ah would ever bevvy sic' a terrible thing! Ye will respect yer mistress!"

Greer fell silent, but kept a defiant gaze at his mistress. Or would she be anymore? He wasn't sure he wanted to keep learning from her if she would lie to him. Perhaps her addiction is why she was an enemy of the Grand Coven in the first place.

"Now ah thought we learned a lesson about assumin' when ah asked ye about 'at frock. Ye didn't think ta politely ask me about ma medicine first?"

Medicine? He knew she usually walked with a cane, having a limp in her right leg whenever she moved. He felt mortified at his behavior, realizing what the cravings for magic had caused him to do. He had acted just like the father he was so afraid of.

He leaped up from his seat, rounding the table before holding his mistress in a tight embrace. "I'm so sorry! I was just thinking about things today, and the magic, and... and..."

"Shh wee pup it's all right! I'm sorry for yellin', I've just never seen ya act 'at way before. I forgive ya darlin'. It's all right..."

Greer knew he would have burst into a sobbing fit without her reasurances, so he gratefully accepted them. What had he been thinking? How could he let those feelings of frustration control his mind?

There was a sudden loud knock at the door that startled them both. Greer heard a vaguely familiar voice yell, "Addison! You will get out here at once!"

Greer was confused, but the ferret had risen into action, gently removing his arms from around her and reaching for her cane. "Get away from th' door will ye?" she bellowed. "Ah don't trust ye there! I'll only meet ye out back!"

"Fine! You best be quick or I'll turn this hut into nothing more than rubble!

Mistress Addison grumbled so quietly Greer could barely hear, "Ah ken just as well as ye do 'at you're na allowed ta knock down a house..." She turned to look directly at Greer. "Come wi' me pup, but bide behin,' all right? Ah want ta keep ye safe."

He nodded, the two then going towards the door. The ferret opened it, revealing no one on the other side. They walked together until they reached the side of the house. Mistress Addison beckoned to him to stay there and keep mostly out of sight. He peeked his maw around the corner only to spot a rabbit drumming a large foot impatiently against the ground, arms crossed.

"Wait... I know her..."

His mistress briefly turned to give him a surprised look, but quickly returned her focus to the hare. "So what do ah owe th' pleasure ay yer company Mistress Charlotte?"

"Oh spare me your false pleasantries! An apprentice? Really? You have already perverted magic with your thievery and yet you decide to encourage the wrath of the Grand Coven further? After we already were so kind as to allow you this hut in the woods at all!"

Greer kept by the house, watching his mistress confidently strut with her limp towards the other witch.

"Are ye spyin' on me now? Ye can listen ta Mistress Elizibeth all ye like but ah stole nothin'. Ah control th' power ay th' ley lines just like anyone of th' damned coven!"

Greer stood stunned. Stealing? He realized he had been so overtaken at his rescue and attempts to find magic that he had never asked why exactly Mistress Addison was considered an enemy of the coven. What if she wasn't the woman he thought he knew? Greer dismissed the thought. He wouldn't fall victim to assumptions again.

The two had been loudly bickering as he worked out his thoughts. He stepped confidently around the corner. "There must be a misunderstanding. Mistress Addison took me in when no one else would. She nursed me back to health and kept me safe. She is a good woman!"

Mistress Addison looked back at him with concern, but also overwhelming pride in her eyes. The look in Mistress Charlotte's eyes went quickly from shock to rage.

"How could you? You lie to the world as it is, but to try and bring some poor boy into your delusions? No... No this is beyond unacceptable!" Without warning, Mistress Charlotte pushed her arm before her with a raised paw, sending a gust of wind intended to knock the two over.

"Greer, gang back around th' house, I'll defend ye!" Mistress Addison stamped her cane onto the ground, the gust of air dissipating into a light breeze before it had the chance to more than billow their clothing. "Bad form Charlotte! All members ay th' coven must arrange a witch's duel before castin' a spell against another witch. Ye ken 'at!"

"You are no member of the coven, nor are you a witch you thief! I will dispatch of you and bring you before Mistress Elizabeth. She will finally put an end to your madness."

Greer scampered back behind the corner of the house, peeking out to get a good view. A magical battle! His heart raced with fear-tinged excitement. He was excited to see his mistress in action but had also seen what she had done to that tree. He didn't want to see her come to any harm. He feared whatever caused her limp could cause her to be overtaken and lose the battle.

The two witches glared at one another, moving slowly, ready for whomever stuck first. His gaze turned to Mistress Addison's footpaws noticing with every step she seemed to drag them across the ground, in almost a circular pattern. It dawned on him that she was searching for a ley line to draw from.

Mistress Charlotte didn't seem to have this problem, deciding to strike again. Her digits curled into fists, arms jabbing at the air. Greer swore he saw orbs filled with swirling wind pummel out with every punch, soaring towards his mistress! She carefully did her best to dodge, mumbling obscenities unintelligibly in her thick accent.

"Hah! What's the matter, not enough stolen power to even attack? Pathetic! We should have ended you long ago."

The hare's ears pulled back, her foot drumming on the ground as she attempted to deal more magical blows. Mistress Addison dodged and weaved around them expertly, slowly drawing closer to her opponent with determination set in her features. It seemed she refused to let the taunting get to her.

This in no way stopped Mistress Charlotte from trying her best to sling insults alongside magic at her foe. "We both know what you are Addison. You cannot hide your being a man any more than you can deny the manhood between your legs!"

Greer was confused. How could the rabbit call her a man when she could clearly see her using magic? Had she somehow stolen magic to become a woman? The thought thrilled Greer, though he couldn't explain why. He could only see the hurt flashing across Mistress Addison's eyes.

"Aww, I struck a chord did I now? You hear that boy? Your so-called mistress is not only a liar, but a man in disguise!"

The ferret had dealt with enough of the rabbit's hateful words. "So focused on ye hate ye haven't realized you're in th' wey o bein' struck upside th' noggin eh?"

The tree, the same one she had clawed to pieces, seemed to groan behind the hare. Mistress Charlotte turned back to study the sound, seeing the tree swinging a massive limb as if to strike her down. She leapt back with a cocky laugh. "Really? That's all you've go-"

The rabbit hadn't considered when leaping back, just how close this would bring her to the very ferret she was fighting. Mistress Addison let her cane land upon the back of her assailant's head with a loud thud, causing her to collapse to the ground unconscious.

Mistress Addison burst into a giggling fit. "Yer first lesson of magical duelin' Greer: most witches forget 'at it doesn't tak' a spell ta defeat them!"

She motioned for him to join her, Greer quickly padding towards her. She knelt down beside the hare, gently placing her two paws around her head.

"M-Mistress Addison, you're n-not going to... kill her are you?"

The ferret once again was laughing. "Ay course na, but if ye burst a head stoaner enough ta cause a nap like this, you've pure hurt somethin'. We have ta heal 'er up ta be sure she's safe! That's why ah didn't use much for spells, didn't want ta be too tired at th end."

"Wait, but she was going to hurt you! Why would you help her now?"

Mistress Addison began a low hum, a gentle breeze flowing past them. She eyed the hare's head in her paws, only stopping her humming when she seemed satisfied. Greer could tell she had healed her in some way, despite the hare remaining asleep.

"It is like th' tree, though different. She attacks, but only coz 'er min' is poisoned by th' ravin' a Mistress Elizabeth." She paused a moment to stand, using her cane for support.

"Know this Greer, na wrong has ever come from defendin' yerself. However, a witch should never seek ta harm. Once witches lacked rules for duels, before Mistress Elizabeth came to rule th' coven. Alas, there's na changin' 'at now. Doesn't mean we have ta act like them though. Come, she will be fine here."

Mistress Addison turned to walk back towards their hut, Greer utterly confused. "Shouldn't we bring her in with us?"

"Na pup. Ah ken this is confusin', but th' coven has rules about enterin' dwellings without permission. Earlier, she showed she would obey them. If ah brin' 'er in, I've 'welcomed 'er ta ma home' an' we lack 'at protection. Come, ah trust she will wake safe an' sound. We still need ta eat."

Greer nodded and did as his mistress instructed. He had forgotten they were about to eat before this commotion began. There were so many questions he wanted to ask. What had she stolen, if anything, from the Grand Coven? Why did they hold such animosity to her when she seemed nothing but kind? What on Earth was Mistress Charlotte going on about her being a man? He felt full to bursting wanting to ask, but after his previous outburst of accusing her of drinking poppy wine, he didn't want to speak out of place again.

The two entered the hut, Mistress Addison lowering herself into her chair at the table with a groan, her ankle obviously bothering her. "Darn thin'..." she grumbled before grabbing the small bottle that had started their previous argument and finishing it with a single swig.

"Mistress Addison...?"

"Aye pup, I'm sure ya have many questions. May ah save us some trouble an' simply tell ye th' why an' how ay th' coven's anger?"

She knew Greer's thoughts before he could even speak them. He nodded in encouragement.

"Thank ye, though ye need ta eat while ah do. Ye still need some meat on yer bones!"

She cracked a smile more melancholy than cheerful. He complied, scooping up some of the now-chilly 'Mushroom Surprise' in a paw. Despite it having grown cold, her cooking was as delicious as ever.

"Now pup, usually a witch will choose 'er an apprentice an' simply teach them magic. Usually, they are quite young. However, there are times th' coven finds someone talented wi' magic, young or old, that somehow stumbled across th' ley lines an' their powers. When they do, they are assigned a witch so they may learn. Na body wants a witch accidentally hurtin' others, unable ta control their magic."

Greer asked, between mawfuls of mushrooms, "So you were one of them?"

"Ah was, sort of at least. Ye may have noticed ah don't gab like many around here?"

He grinned, trying his best to imitate her. "Ya don' say?"

A grin spread across her maw, ears perking up for the first time since their interruption earlier. "Cheeky pup! But aye, I'm na from here." The ferret's entire body seemed to droop in sorrow. "Pup, please don't think poorly ah me. Ah only wish ta bide th' life ah know ah must. Ah never intend ta deceive nor hurt. Ah simply need ta be myself, do ya understand? Ah wasn't named Addison at birth, this is th' name ah chose for myself."

"Mistress Addison, I've known others to change their name, why would that be shameful in any way? If you had a hard past, I can't blame you!"

The ferret sighed, resting her face within her paws. "Greer, ye don' truly understand. When ah was born, mah mum n' dah thought they had conceived a boy."

Greer was taken aback. "How? You look nothing like one? Wait, does this have something to do with what Mistress Charlotte said?"

She nodded glumly. "See, all th' parts ah had matched up, but they didn't match my mind. Mah folks weren't keen an' tried ta hush me when I brought it up even as a child.

When ah got close ta yer age my body grew as

a young male ferret's would, far larger than mah feminine kin. Mah voice grew lower, rough, an ah felt as though mah own body was betrayin' me. That's why I brewed what was in those bottles."

The medicine she took each day made her look the way she did? He saw how her features seemed softer than most males, her chest with the curves all women he knew had. He had even seen the steady sway of her hips as she limped along in times prior. He couldn't picture the ferret as anything but a woman. From her actions to appearance there was no doubt to him. Greer would never have known had Mistress Addison had not been forced to explain.

"Wait, so you have, what I have. Um, down there, yes?" He was mortified to ask the question, feeling his cheeks warm as he averted his gaze.

Mistress Addison could not hide her amusement despite the seriousness of the situation. "Aye pup, yes."

Greer was quick to move on, too flustered to continue this line of reasoning. "Was this what they thought you stole from them then? This potion to become a woman?"

"First pup, I was always a lass. These just help mah outer shell look like mah inner shell. Second, ah came up wi' these when ah was still at home, in secret. Ah knew 'at folks wouldn't understand, but ah had ta bide mah dream, mah true self. So ah ran away ta start mah transformation, mah new life."

The thought of just how fantastic a transformation it was still floored him. Sure, he had seen the rat in his story become a princess, but that had taken magic and miracles. Could something as simple as drinking a small bottle of herbs at a meal change someone so thoroughly?

"So that's what brought you here, but why do they think you've stolen something? It's obvious you can perform magic Mistress."

"Mistress Charlotte said it was obvious too once I showed her. See, when ah came ta this town, ah learned about witches an' their magic. Ah was eavesdroppin' on witches' conversations, when I heard th' bunny speakin' of th' ley lines. Ah thought ah would try ta fin' them, an' after many times, ah succeeded! Ah showed Mistress Charlotte an' she was so excited ta tak me ta th' coven an' fin' someone ta teach me. I was overwhelmed wi' joy. Till' they found mah bottles, just as ye did."

The rat could see the emotions playing out across the ferret's body, the lofty high only to be met by a crushing low. A feeling he knew he had once felt all too well himself. Greer reached out, offering his paw for her to grip in her own. She gladly took it for support.

"When ah was honest an' told them how it helped mah bein' the woman I am... Hell broke loose. I didn't know 'at only women could perform magic, just like ye didn't. To Mistress Charlotte, what was between mah legs meant there was no way ah could do magic. Ah was branded an enemy ay th' coven, forced ta leave town an' build this hut ta support myself. Been here for years, only going to town ta get things th' forest won't provide."

"Ah understand if ye feel ya can't trust me now. It's

a big thin' ta keep from ya, but ah was afraid. Ah only want ta be treated like myself. It is all ah ask for, ta bide life an' be happy."

He considered his mistress a moment, reflecting on the dissonance he sometimes felt with his own body and how different he felt from other young boys he knew. She held such conviction of her womanhood she stood even against the Grand Coven. Did any of what she said change anything? She was still the kind woman he knew. The woman who had seen his spark and desire to learn magic and offered to help despite the risks. So what if she was different? He was too. Perhaps the conviction of one's womanhood came from the soul and not the body.

"Mistress Addison, this changes nothing. In all the time I've known you, you have but wonderful. You are a good person and don't need to explain yourself to me! If you say you are a woman, to me you are and nothing will change my min—"

It was the ferret's turn to leap from her seat for a hug. Before Greer could finish his sentence she wrapped him in a warm embrace, squeezing him tightly as tears poured from her eyes. "Greer, ah knew ah was right ta tak' ye on as an apprentice!"

Greer savored the hug. His father nor his mother had ever been much for physical affection. His chest swelled with pride that someone who had overcome such struggles as she had would find him such a worthy apprentice.

The tender moment was interrupted by a groan from outside the cabin. "Ay, ah think th' bunny is wakin'."

"Should we go back out to her?"

Mistress Addison released the rat from her embrace. "Nah pup, she'd just start swingin' again. Let 'er stomp off an' cool down. Na need ta let 'er disturb our happy home any longer."

Greer smiled up at her. "It's a deal, as long as you eat some too. I can't let you get as skinny as me!"

The pure joy resonating from her laugh made Greer's tail wag in response. "All right pup, but I prefer mah meal hot!" With a small grin she touched a single digit of her paw to the food and in a short moment it was steaming as though it had just been freshly cooked.

"What! That's no fair, why didn't you reheat mine?"

"Ya didn't ask!"

The mustelid and rodent both laughed together. The ferret promised her apprentice she would teach him that trick, but only if he would begin learning how to forage and cook from the woods. The bargain was struck, and the two enjoyed the delicious mushrooms before them until weariness overcame them, forcing them to slumber.

5

When morning came, the two checked outside just to be sure that Mistress Charlotte had left, feeling relief when she was no longer there. The next few days were bliss. Greer felt as though he had never been closer with anyone than his mistress as she took him through the woods, helping him learn ways to identify which plants were safe to eat.

She took an even more hands-on approach to his learning than before as well. With a helping hand to cook, they would have time after dinner for her to come help him find the ley lines. She would shuffle her feet as she had during the duel, instructing Greer to copy. Whenever she found a strong ley line, she would direct him to it while offering encouragement and advice to try and sense its power.

Each attempt was met with returning thoughts of

the day he was forced from his home. Mistress Addison told him time and again that he would need a mind clear with nothing but his purpose to succeed. Yet he would attempt to place these thoughts aside only for them to return with greater vigor. While frustrated that his attempts had so far borne no results, he appreciated the time spent with Mistress Addison.

He even found the urges to desperately search further were beginning to subside. He no longer wished to sneak out at night. The weather had begun to cool further at night, and Mistress Addison had suggested they cuddle close during sleep to keep warm with their combined fur and heat. She had told him leaving a fire going overnight in her hut wasn't the safest idea.

Among the rats he had grown up with, this was a normal practice among families as buying fuel for overnight fires was an expense left only for those who could afford it. He had always been forced to the outside of the pile in his home, but with Mistress Addison it was different.

He felt such affection when she gently wrapped her arms around him each evening. He wouldn't trade that feeling of comfort for a fleeting chance at the magic he longed to feel once again. He felt he belonged here more than he ever had anywhere before and relished the joy it brought him.

Here he was free to be himself, to find joy as he learned each new letter, each new plant, and felt no fear in expressing his feelings. Mistress Addison appreciated his curiosity for the world like nobody he had known before. She had even encouraged him to tie back the ever growing mop of fur on his head with a ribbon when he asked if he could. She even allowed him to pick any color he wished, and was thrilled when he chose pink.

Be it blinded by bliss or simply surprised, neither had expected the ball of flame to rocket at them out of the woods one evening as they practiced finding the ley lines.

"Greer, watch it!"

Mistress Addison had dove upon him, the two falling to the ground just in time to avoid the flame that careened into a tree, but oddly vanished instead of causing it to burst alight. A cat with fur as black as her robes marched solemnly from the woods, green eyes burning with rage.

"Mistress Charlotte has informed me you will not give up these whims that you are a woman and refuse to relinquish your apprentice. I refuse to allow you to play these games any longer. Relinquish your apprentice who stands no chance to learn and give me whatever object you have stolen magic with and I will let the two of you live."

Mistress Addison's body shook with a rage Greer had not thought her capable of. She gave him a glance to be sure he was okay before removing herself from on top of him, rising with the aid of her cane.

"Ye bloody dobber, ye could have killed us!"

The woman's expression did not change, only the irritated twitching of her tail betrayed her true feelings. Greer trembled in fear. He had never seen something as destructive as fire controlled before. Realization dawned upon him. Only someone who was truly a master of magic could control such a force. This must be Mistress Elizibeth.

"I repeat! Relinquish your apprentice and stolen magic, and I will allow the two of you the privilege of breathing another day!"

The ferret spat onto the ground before whispering, "Greer, get somewhere safe..."

He hadn't had a moment to even move before another ball of flame was whirling towards them. Mistress Addison swiped her free paw through the air, summoning magical force to bat it away with a yell of fury.

"It's the cane!" Mistress Elizibeth's eyes glowed as though she had realized a great truth. She thrust both her paws forward, flames erupting from them towards her ferret foe. Greer scrambled desperately out of the way, Mistress Addison flung both of her arms in front of her face, deflecting the flames but being thrown violently backwards.

"Mistress!"

The black cat growled at Greer. "You shall not use that term! That is for witches, women of magic. Not a man!"

Mistress Elizabeth moved her paw as if to strike him with magic. Despite the injuries she had surely sustained from her forceful fall, the ferret flew from the ground. A powerful wind blew through the branches as she was propelled with great force towards the rat.

"Ye will not harm him!" she cried out, clawing

through the air once again. The black cat stopped whatever forces she had mustered with a simple flick of her wrist. While Mistress Addison was already desperately panting, her foe didn't appear to have exerted an iota of energy.

"Fool, you never learned how to properly wield magic, to store power in objects for future use! Whoever you stole from wouldn't have taught you, would she?"

The black cat slung more fire at the ferret. Mistress Addison desperately attempted to try and swat them away, but was quickly overcome, stumbling backwards on the ground next to Greer. He could smell the panic in her musk even through smoky, singed fur.

Mistress Elizabeth flew forward without hesitation, curling a paw upwards. A powerful gust came from the ground, snatching the cane from the mustelid's weakened grasp as it rocketed towards the cat. Upon reaching her paw she took the cane as dark as her fur and snapped it in half across her knee, tossing the two pieces aside.

"Relinquish your apprentice, scum, or you will know just how kind I have been with my flames." An unearthly glow seemed to be forming around her as though she were cloaked in a magical inferno.

Mistress Addison raised her head, doing her best to look at her assailant with her one eye not swollen beyond its ability to see from the fight. She spat blood from her maw, Greer feared she had been far more injured than even he had expected.

"Ah would rather die. Greer isn't just an apprentice.

Greer is mah kin! Ah need no cane ta kick yer bloody arse. Fight me fair, hen ta hen, in a proper duel!"

Cruel sarcasm dripped from every laugh pouring forth from the black cat's maw. "Woman to woman? A woman connects to the Earth Mother in a way no man can. She births magic into this world so that only those who can give birth themselves can control her power. The only thing you have given birth to are deceptions and delusions."

The ferret coughed, blood splattering on the earth before her. She turned sorrowfully towards Greer. "Please run pup. Ah could na bear ta see ye harmed..."

She thrust out a paw, unable to push him away with magic in her weary state, relying on force to do the job. He stumbled backwards, frozen, unable to do her bidding.

"Ah said run! Ye swore ta follow mah every instruction an' ah am intructin' ye ta run!"

"Pitiful, a true witch could defend her mistress. This entire partnership is as built on deceit as it is fantasy. Yet you refuse to relinquish your apprentice! As Headmistress of the Grand Coven, I sentence you to death!"

As Mistress Elizibeth made her decree, the ferret tried to fight back. She could barely raise a paw before concussive force slammed it aside. Greer could hear a sickening pop followed by the agonized cry of his mistress.

"Accept your fate!" Mistress Elizibeth raised a paw, a massive globe of flame quickly forming before her, preparing to deal a final blow.

In that moment, time stood still in Greer's mind. There were no tricks left up his mistress's sleeve. No cane to suddenly swing at a head, even if she had the strength to do so. No tree to do her bidding and surprise her assailant. No hope.

He saw Mistress Addison, a crumpled heap on the ground, struggling for breath between sobs of pain. The woman who had saved him from starvation, given him purpose, shown him love he had never before known. He had to protect her as she had him. If ever there was a moment for magic, it was now.

He scrambled to his foot paws, taking the stance the ferret had taught him, trying with all his might to once again feel the flow of power coursing through him.

The black cat caught his movement, his attempts eliciting more of her raucous scorn. "Pathetic boy, have you learned nothing this evening? Only a woman may do magic! You may be a sissy weakling, but you do not qualify!"

That word, sissy. It was almost as though the cruel witch somehow knew the perfect thing to say that would antagonize him. His thoughts quickly raced, remembering that fateful day, remembering the agony he would be returned to if Mistress Addison was no longer a part of his life. No more love, no more acceptance. The one person who had respected his privacy in what he wore and had only spoken poorly of it from true concern, not of hatred. The woman that wanted, above all else, for Greer to be true to himself.

Still, all that could spring to his mind was the damn

dress! Greer was startled to feel the gentlest glow of warmth flooding through his body. The dress, Greer had never accepted just how much they had loved the dress.

An' above all else, do ye swear ta be true ta yerself?

Her words rang out through Greer's thoughts. He could not not feel the magic because he was not being true to himself!

No, she was not being true to herself.

An ear-splitting crack of thunder rang through the air with such force even the composed Mistress Elizabeth lost focus on her spell, the flames sputtering out. Greer felt the static of magic rippling through her veins once more, yearning to burst forth like fabulous fireworks at her command. She had found the magic! She could sense the ley lines permeating the earth beneath her footpaws. She positioned herself over the strongest one she could find, unsure of how to control the power surging through her.

I must save Mistress Addison! Lightning crackled within her paws, a force so powerful she could barely contain it. The black cat's jaw had dropped in alarm, her body quaking in fear.

"Y-You, boy! How h-have you stolen th-this—"

She did not allow Mistress Elizabeth to finish speaking, a bolt of plasma zipping through the air a hair's breadth from the feline. Mistress Elizabeth fell to her knees, tail thrashing, aware of how much danger she found herself in.

"I have stolen nothing! You are the Headmistress, you are supposed to be wise! Not needing to be taught by a child. The person one is has nothing to do with their appearance, but with who they are inside! If a cinder-covered maid may be seen as a princess, you can see my mistress as the woman she is!"

"N-No! What trickery is this? I broke the cane that stored the power! Even I cannot control lightning! " She rose to stand again, but pure light flashed through the sky once more, causing her to return to cower in fear.

"I have seen my mistress rend a tree to nothing but splinters without ever holding that cane and grow it back to full form. I have seen what kindness magic can bring this world and know you have no part in it. We both can use magic, and you will either accept the truth of our womanhood or be struck down by righteous justice!"

For the first time in her life Mistress Elizabeth was experiencing how the terror she brought others could feel. She curled into a ball on the ground, pathetic, begging for mercy.

"You will leave! You will tell all in your coven the truth about my mistress. If you ever return to bring harm to either of us, I will be sure my strikes do not miss!"

The cat wept in response, scrambling to her hands and knees to scamper away. He had never seen an adult actually run on all fours, something usually reserved for young children playing, but found great joy in seeing her flee this way.

"Greer...?"

Mistress Elizabeth had scrambled from sight.

The weak moan of her mistress caused Greer to lose grip on the power she was controlling, the lightning dissipating as quickly as it had come.

"Mistress Addison!"

Greer ran to her, cradling the ferret's much larger frame in her far smaller arms. She was badly injured, but besides herbs, she knew of no way to help her.

"Greer, I am sa sorry..."

Her ears twitched with confusion. "What could you be sorry about? You kept me safe, I should be sorry I couldn't help you sooner!"

Despite her pain the ferret chuckled. "For callin' ye a pup. You've been a kit all along. I'm sa sorry, ye deserve th' respect you've shown me."

Greer couldn't help but laugh. As her mistress sat in pain, arm mangled, she still only thought of showing proper kindness. "I didn't even know myself, at least not all the way yet. It's fine, but you are not. How do I heal you? Can I even heal you? I don't know how I even summoned that lightning..."

Mistress Addison rested her head against Greer's chest, releasing a pained sigh. "Draw upon th' power. Let it wash through ye, bend it ta yer will, command it ta nourish, ta mend, ta heal. It will listen ta a kin' soul like yours."

Greer attempted her best to do as she was instructed, crying tears of worry as she tried. She didn't want to lose Mistress Addison, she was afraid she would do something wrong. She could feel the power waning, her emotions overtaking her ability to control it.

Thankfully, it seemed the ferret was at least stable.

Her arm had returned to normal and her eye was no longer as swollen. Even if she still smelled of burnt fur Greer didn't care. She clung tightly to her mistress in love and relief.

"I love you Mistress Addison. I cannot lose you. You still have so much to teach me."

The ferret cracked a worn out grin. "Aye, like how bad those brews ah concoct taste. If ay course ye want ta try em'. Figured ye might after realizin' today."

Greer burst into laughter. Even in her battered state, Mistress Addison couldn't help but tease and joke. No matter what injuries her body had sustained, she knew the ferret's good nature had not been damaged.

"Yes, I think I'd like that very much!"

Greer assisted the ferret to her feet, helping her keep balance as her weakened body trembled.

"Do you think we can get you back into the house?"

Mistress Addison's tail swished mischievously. "Aye, mah legs are only shakin' from th' power ay yer poetry. From cinders ta princess eh? Wasn't 'at a wee bit much?"

The two joined in laugher, Greer helping her mistress hobble into her hut. The rat would be able to return the favor she had been given, to nurse her mistress back to health. She needed the ferret at full strength as she knew she had much to learn. Not just of magic, but more of herself.

Content Warning

This book contains transphobic language and themes of addiction.

Linnea is a bubbly ball of fluff with an insatiable wanderlust. When not seeking out adventures and experiences, she happily plays songs on her ukulele and writes the stories she dreams up every night before bed.

Twitter: @LiteralGrill
www.linneacapps.com

## Coming Soon to Weasel Press

*Going Somewhere* by Joe 3.0
*Book of Beasts* by Holly Day
*The Moon Crawls on All Fours* by Robin Gow
*My Name Does Not Belong to Me* by Luke Kuzmish
*Things for Which You Thirst* by Claudine Nash
*Dire Moon Cartoons* by John Sullivan
*Nothing Nice to Say* by Stephanie Webber
*Once More with Noise* by Weasel

## OTHER TITLES FROM WEASEL PRESS

*Pan's Saxophone* by Jonel Abellanosa

*Klonopin Meets Sisyphus* by Adam Levon Brown

*Bleeding Saffron* by David E. Cowen

*Face Down in the Leaves* by Dwale

*In Winter's Dreams We Wake* by Ryan Quinn Flanagan

*Just Under the Sky* by RK Gold

*If the Hero of Time was Black* by Ashley Harris

*In and of Blood* by Kat Lewis

*I Am A Terrorist* by Sarah Frances Moran

*Death & Heartbreak* by Leah Mueller

*Lipstick Stained Masculinity* by Mason O'Hern

*Viscera* by Manna Plourde

*UHAUL: A Collection of Lesbian Love Poems* by Emily Ramser

*The Escape* by Rayah

*Miffed and Peeved in the UK* by Neil S. Reddy

*Inevitable* by Amy L. Sasser

*Satan's Sweethearts* by Marge Simon and Mary Turzillo

*Passing Through* edited by Weasel

*Wolf: An Epic and Other Poems* by Z.M. Wise

CPSIA information can be obtained
at www.ICGtesting.com
Printed in the USA
LVHW010716100820
662780LV00005B/330